The Big Beautiful Purple Tree

Brian McKanna

This book is dedicated to the love of my life, my wonderful wife, Kat.

Also to my always supportive family the McKanna's, the Miller's, and the Ely's.

I'd like to give special thanks to my Dad for encouraging me to share this story with the world. Without your help this book would have never come to be.

Once upon a time there was a little town nestled in the quiet

foothills of the Ozark Mountains known as Green Pines.

On one side of town there was a vast forest so thick with foliage that moss coated everything beneath the canopy. On the other side, the rolling foothills meandered up and down gently cradling the quaint town.

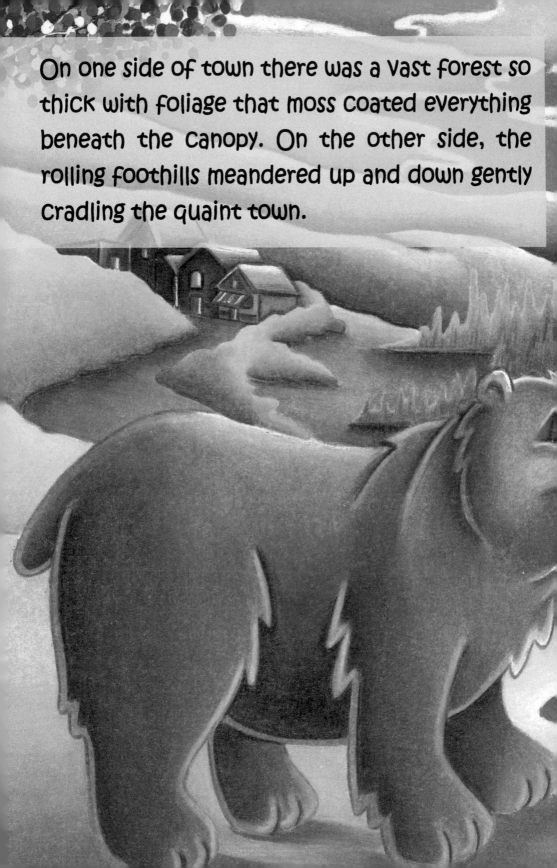

Green Pines, at first glance, appeared no different than the next town in the Ozark Mountain range, yet there was something extraordinary about it.

Atop the highest foothill overlooking the town was a lone tree, the most magnificent big beautiful purple tree you could ever lay your eyes upon!

Unlike any ordinary tree, every inch of bark and limb and leaf upon it had a hue of purple that was mesmerizing in appearance!

The townspeople adored the purple tree. Some would sit beneath it as the sun greeted them for an early good morning.

Others, perhaps the younger and more nimble inhabitants of the town would visit the grand tree, climbing its sturdy branches to find the perfect limb to play upon in the afternoons.

Then, as the sun was setting, casting it's last shadows of the day, the town would pause to take in the most glorious shades of purple cascading over Green Pines' square.

Green Pines was a lumber town that always smelled of pine, as you can imagine.

There were three lumberjacks who controlled and maintained the massive forest on the opposite end of town from the purple tree. . .

. . .watching for the biggest and best trees to reach their fullest and then choping them down to make furniture, new homes, or anything else the town folks needed.

They honored the forest by planting new trees in exchange for the old trees they took.

Then came a day when one of the lumberjacks climbed the highest foothill to speak with the lone special tree.

"Excuse me, big beautiful purple tree, I see you're getting older and while your branches and trunk are still in their prime, may I cut you down and make you into some fine benches to put around town? They would get a lot of use" the lumberjack said.

"No!" the great tree replied, "I want to be set free to live amongst the trees in the forest I see beyond the village."

The lumberjack could not argue with the tree's decision, so he turned and headed back down to town.

The next day, the second lumberjack climbed the highest foothill to speak with the massive tree.

"Greetings, big beautiful purple tree," he began, "You are so healthy and strong, your color is unlike any other tree here in Green Pines, may I chop you down and make you into a house for my daughter? She would love to live in a sturdy house of purple wood that only you could provide."

"No!!" the great tree boomed, "I want to be set free to live amongst the trees."

Disappointed, the second lumberjack left the tree and headed back down to town.

The following day, the third lumberjack climbed the hill to speak with the impressive tree.

"Big beautiful purple tree, I have heard your desire. May I set you free to live amongst the trees?" he asked.

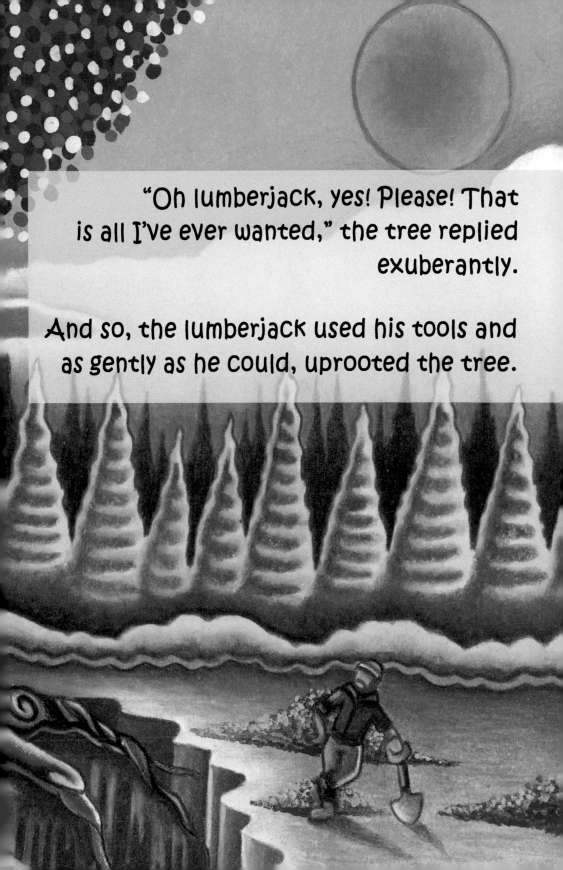

"Oh lumberjack, yes! Please! That is all I've ever wanted," the tree replied exuberantly.

And so, the lumberjack used his tools and as gently as he could, uprooted the tree.

As soon as the purple tree was free from the ground it picked up its roots and sprinted full speed toward the town of Green Pines.

It tore down Main Street with its branches shaking wildly while dirt and rocks flew off its exposed roots, leaving a trail of its happy exit; it bolted deep into the thick forest on the other side of town, never to be seen again.

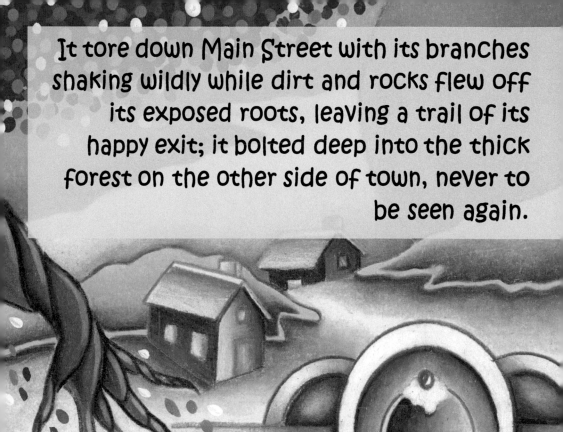

For months thereafter, the people of Green Pines missed their beloved, big beautiful purple tree. No one climbed the hill for sunrise.

The kids did not go up the hill because there were no branches to play upon. The town no longer had purple hues highlighting the streets at sunset.

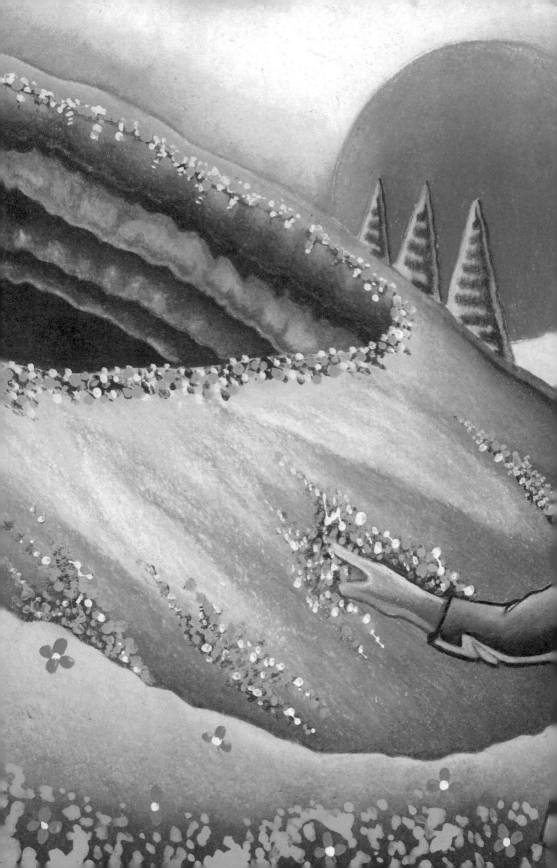

And although the townsfolk were happy the tree got its wish, they were very sad and never forgot how special the big beautiful purple tree was to them and their town.

Until one day it happened. . .

After the first rains of spring, little purple sprouts began poking up and popping out all over, along the path the magnificent purple tree had run including the highest foothill, down Main Street, and the road out of town!

The big beautiful purple tree had received its desire to live amongst the trees and in turn, it gave the town what it wanted too—the everlasting gift of hundreds of seeds that blossomed over the years into hundreds of trees that bathed the village in purple.

Now people would come from miles around to sit beneath their favorite purple tree, children would once again climb to play on beautiful purple branches, and no one would leave before walking through shadows of purple sunsets.

Now, if you ever wanted to visit the Ozark Mountains and went in search of the quiet town called Green Pines that was nestled between a thick forest and meandering foothills, you would not find it.

There is no such place with that name anymore for it was

changed many years ago to its appropriate name, Purple Pines.

Made in the USA
Columbia, SC
03 September 2021